ie and Only
Sparkella
and the
Big Lie

CHANNING TATUM

Illustrated by KIM BARNES

Feiwel and Friends

New York

A FEIWEL AND FRIENDS BOOK
An imprint of Macmillan Publishing Group, LLC
120 Broadway, New York, NY 10271 · mackids.com

Our books may be purchased in bulk for promotional, educational, or business use.
Please contact your local bookseller or the Macmillan Corporate and Premium Sales Department
at (800) 221-7945 ext. 5442 or by email at MacmillanSpecialMarkets@macmillan.com.

Library of Congress Cataloging-in-Publication Data is available.

First edition, 2023
Book design by Sharismar Rodriguez and Lisa Vega
Feiwel and Friends logo designed by Filomena Tuosto
Printed in China by RR Donnelley Asia Printing Solutions Ltd., Dongguan City, Guangdong Province

ISBN 978-1-250-75077-8 (hardcover)
10 9 8 7 6 5 4 3 2 1
ISBN 978-1-250-90669-4 (special edition)
10 9 8 7 6 5 4 3 2 1

To my glitter poop: I love you!!
—Dad

To AP with gratitude
from CHC

There's a new kid in our class whose name is Wyatt. He has the *coolest* sense of style—I mean, look at how awesome that poncho is! And those retro-tastic glasses! Plus, he has a gorgeous singing voice, and he's extra gentle with the class chameleon.

I really want to be his friend. And today, I get my chance, because my dad and his mom have organized a playdate for us.

I was worried Wyatt wouldn't have a good time, though. What do boys even like to do?

All my stuff . . .
well . . .

I didn't know what to do!

But then I had an idea. Tam, my bestest friend in
the whole wide world, has tons of cool toys.
But the *coolest* one is her remote-controlled car.

I knew if I had that car, Wyatt would want to be friends with me. So, when she wasn't looking . . .

I decided to borrow it.

The morning of my playdate,
Tam races over to me at school.

I don't like to see my best friend so upset, and I guess my stomach doesn't, either, because it starts to feel all icky.

"Uh . . . maybe you just misplaced it?"
I say, even though I know she did not.

No,
we looked
everywhere—
it's gone!

Well, uh, maybe . . . maybe the monster in your closet took it?

But he didn't take it forever, he's just borrowing it and is going to return it really soon. I bet.

At this, Tam's sobs turn into wails.

My favorite toy is gone AND I have a monster in my closet?! It's even worse than I thought.

Just then, the bell rings, which is good, because it stops me from telling any more lies.

All day, I watch as the **SPARKLE** drains out of Tam.

At recess, she barely moves at all.

At lunch, she just pushes her bún chả around with her chopsticks.

And in art class, she only uses shades of gray in her painting.

By the end of the day, I feel icky, oogy, and blech. When I look in the mirror, I can see that I've lost all my SPARKLE, too.

When Dad picks me up, he must be able to tell I don't feel good.

It's the first true thing I've said all day.

The sooner I have my playdate with
Wyatt, the sooner I can return Tam's car.

Wyatt arrives at my house
right on time. When I show
him my room, his eyes light up
in wonder.

I'm happy that Wyatt likes my stuff, but what I really want is for him to play with Tam's car.

"I insist!" I say, pushing the toy in his direction.

Maybe later.

My body starts to feel hot. I scream:

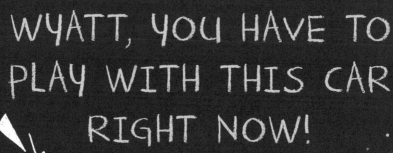

That's when Dad walks in.

I want to tell him the truth, but
instead another lie slips out.

Dad walks over to my toy chest and picks something up.

You mean this Pocket Penny?

And then another lie slips out.

I meant to say that Tam gave it to me. As a present.

Dad gives me a look like he doesn't believe me. And another lie slips out. Actually, more like a gazillion lies.

Now both Dad and Wyatt are looking at me like they don't believe me. My lip starts to tremble, and my eyes do that thing where they preload the tears.

I can't let Wyatt see me cry—then he'll never want to be friends with me. So I quietly get up, walk out of the room . . .

. . . and lock myself in the bathroom.

Why did I tell so many lies? Tam is never going to forgive me, and once Wyatt finds out the truth, he'll *never* want to be friends with me.

And Dad! He's going to be so angry. I bet he's about to call the police. I stole Tam's car, which makes me a *criminal*.

LAUNDRY

The tears that were
preloaded start to fall.

KNOCK KNOCK!

There's a knock at the door.
I can tell it's Dad,
so I let him in.

Sparky, is there something you want to tell me?

He asks all soft and gentle,
which makes me want to
cry even harder.

A bunch of lies fill my brain,
but I decide to tell the truth.

With that, he takes out his phone and dials a number.

On the way there, I apologize to Wyatt for yelling at him and interrupting our playdate. He is very gracious, which means he sweetly accepts my apology. He even asks if I want to come over to his house on Saturday.

We arrive at Tam's house, and it feels like a whole kaleidoscope of butterflies has moved into my tummy.

I take the car out of my backpack, and Tam's face squishes in confusion.

I breathe in 1 - 2 - 3 - 4

and out 1 - 2 - 3 - 4.

And when I'm done . . . I tell the truth.

Tam is quiet, but just for a moment.
"That's okay," Tam says, because she
is also gracious. "I forgive you."

This time, I breathe a deep sigh
of relief, and I hug my best friend,
who squeezes me back. I feel my
SPARKLE return.

Wyatt walks up to us.

Hey, Tam! Sparkella is coming over this weekend. You can come, too, if you want.

It'd be nice to have another new friend.

When he says the magical "friend" word, I feel myself go from sparkly to DAZZLING.